Giggle, Giggle, Quack

ARTIST'S NOTE

For this book I did brush drawings using Winsor & Newton lamp black watercolor on tracing paper. I then had the drawings photocopied onto one-ply Strathmore kid finish watercolor paper and applied watercolor washes to the black drawings. The advantage to this method is that I can get as many copies on the watercolor paper as I want, and I can experiment with the color, choosing the finishes that I like the best.

ISBN 0-439-52153-X

Text copyright © 2002 by Doreen Cronin. Illustrations copyright © 2002 by Betsy Lewin. All rights reserved. Published by Scholastic Inc., 557 Broadway, New York, NY 10012, by arrangement with Simon & Schuster Books for Young Readers, Simon & Schuster Children's Publishing Division. SCHOLASTIC and associated logos are trademarks and/or registered trademarks of Scholastic Inc.

12 11 10 9 8 7 6 5 4 3 2   3 4 5 6 7 8/0

Printed in the U.S.A.   10

First Scholastic printing, September 2003

Book Design by Anahid Hamparian

The text of this book is set in 30-point Filosofia Bold.

For Andrew

—D. C.

For Rosanne Lauer

—B. L.

Giggle, Giggle, Quack

by Doreen Cronin   pictures by Betsy Lewin

SCHOLASTIC INC.

New York Toronto London Auckland Sydney
Mexico City New Delhi Hong Kong Buenos Aires

Farmer Brown was going on vacation. He left his brother, Bob, in charge of the animals.

"I wrote everything down for you. Just follow my instructions and everything will be fine. But keep an eye on Duck. He's trouble."

Farmer Brown thought he heard
giggles and snickers as he drove
away, but he couldn't be sure.

Bob gave Duck a good long stare
and went inside.
He read the first note:

Tuesday night
is pizza night
(not the frozen
kind!).
The hens prefer
anchovies.

Giggle, giggle, cluck.

Twenty-nine minutes later
there was hot pizza in the barn.

Bob checked on the animals
before he went to bed.
Everything was just fine.

Wednesday is bath day
for the pigs.
Wash them with my
favorite bubble bath and
dry them off with my
good towels.
Remember, they have
very sensitive skin.

Giggle, giggle, oink.

Bob had all the pigs washed in no time.

Farmer Brown called home on Wednesday night to check in. "Did you feed the animals like I wrote in the note?" he asked.

"Done," replied Bob, counting seven empty pizza boxes.

"Did you see my note about the pigs?"
"All taken care of," said Bob proudly.

"Are you keeping a very close eye on Duck?" he asked.

Bob gave Duck a good long stare. Duck was too busy sharpening his pencil to notice.

"Just keep him in the house,"
ordered Farmer Brown.
"He's a bad influence on the cows."

Giggle, giggle, moo, giggle,
oink, giggle, quack.

Giggle, giggle, moo.

Bob was in the kitchen, popping corn.
Just as the animals settled in to watch
THE SOUND OF MOOSIC, the phone rang.

The only thing Farmer Brown heard on the other end was:

"Giggle, giggle, quack, giggle, moo, giggle, oink. . . ."

UH-OH.

"DUCK!"

screamed Farmer Brown.